# JANE EYRE

ORIGINAL BY CHARLOTTE BRONTË

RETOLD BY PAULINE FRANCIS

EVANS BROTHERS LIMITED

Published by Evans Brothers Limited
2A Portman Mansions
Chiltern Street
London W1U 6NR

© Evans Brothers Limited 2005
First published 2005

Printed in Hong Kong

British Library Cataloguing in Publication data
Francis, Pauline
        Jane Eyre
        1.Governesses - England - Juvenile fiction   2. England -
        Social life and customs - 19th century - Juvenile fiction
        3. Children's stories
        I. Title. II. Bronte, Charlotte, 1816-1855. Jane Eyre
        823.9'14 [J]

ISBN 0 237 52687 5

# JANE EYRE

**CHAPTER ONE**  *Terror in the Red Room*

**CHAPTER TWO**  *Lowood School*

**CHAPTER THREE**  *A Cry in the Attic*

**CHAPTER FOUR**  *Fire! Fire!*

**CHAPTER FIVE**  *An Unwelcome Visitor*

**CHAPTER SIX**  *Forgive and Forget*

**CHAPTER SEVEN**  *The Face in the Candlelight*

**CHAPTER EIGHT**  *Alone*

**CHAPTER NINE**  *A Voice in the Dark*

**CHAPTER TEN**  *"Reader, I married him!"*

# *Introduction*

Charlotte Brontë was born in 1816 in Yorkshire, in the north of England. When she was four years old, her father became the vicar of Haworth, a small town on the Yorkshire Moors. Charlotte's mother died a year after they moved and their aunt came to look after the five children. When Charlotte was eight, she was sent away to school with Maria and Elizabeth, two of her sisters. Her sisters died at the school.

After leaving school Charlotte became a governess and a teacher, spending some time in Belgium. But she always missed her beloved moors when she was away.

Charlotte Brontë wrote *Jane Eyre* in 1847, under the name Currer Bell, as novels by women were not often published. It tells the story of the orphan Jane Eyre who becomes a governess at Thornfield Hall. Here she falls in love with its owner, Mr Rochester – and discovers his terrible secret.

Charlotte Brontë wrote three other novels: *Shirley* (1849), *Villette* (1853) and *The Professor* (published in 1857 after her death). But *Jane Eyre* is the most popular because it was one of the first novels to tell a story from a young child's point of view. Jane Eyre is only ten when her story begins.

Charlotte Brontë did marry, but died a year later in 1855, at the age of thirty-nine.

## CHAPTER ONE

# Terror in the Red Room

My cousins – Eliza, John and Georgina Reed – were sitting with their mother by the fire. I was not allowed to join them, so I took a book and went to read by the window. But John found me there. John Reed was fourteen years old, four years older than me. He was large for his age and he bullied me all the time. I trembled in terror every time he came near me.

"You have no right to read our books," he said, snatching it from me. "You have no money and no parents. You ought to beg, not live here with gentleman's children like us."

He threw the book at me and I fell, hitting my head against the door.

"Wicked and cruel boy!" I shouted, as the blood trickled down my face.

He ran straight at me, and pulled my hair. My aunt and Bessie, the nurse, forced us apart.

"Lock her in the red room!" my aunt cried.

I struggled all the way upstairs. In the red room, Bessie sat me on a stool and stood staring at me. "You must remember, Jane Eyre," she said, "that if your aunt decided to turn you out of this house, you would end up in the poor-house."

I did not reply. I had heard it all before.

"I am telling you this for your own good," Bessie continued. "You must try to be useful and pleasant. Then you would be welcome here at Gateshead Hall."

She left, locking the door behind her. The red room was a spare room. It was cold because there was hardly ever a fire – and silent because it was a long way from the nursery. But worst of all, this was the room in which my uncle, Mr Reed, had died nine years ago.

I went to see if the door was really locked. Alas! Yes! As I returned to my stool, I walked in front of a large mirror. I gazed at my white face and arms gleaming in the gloom, at my eyes glittering with fear. I looked like a ghost.

Daylight began to fade. It was now past four o'clock and the rain was still beating against the windows. I grew as cold as a stone and I began to feel afraid. I tried to remember my uncle – my mother's brother – who had taken me in when I was orphaned. As he lay dying, he had made his wife promise to bring me up as one of her own children.

"If my uncle was still alive, he would have treated me kindly," I thought.

I tried hard to be brave, until I saw a light gleaming on the wall. Then it moved across the ceiling. My heart started to beat faster. I gave a long and wild cry until I heard footsteps and the key turning in the lock.

"Miss Eyre, are you ill?" Bessie asked.

"I saw a light," I cried. "I thought it was a ghost! Let me out!"

"What is going on?" It was my aunt. "I gave orders that Jane Eyre should be left in the red room until I decided she should come out."

"Oh, aunt, have pity!" I cried. "Forgive me! I cannot bear it."

But my aunt pushed me back into the room and locked the door again. Then I fainted.

I woke up much later in my own room. No severe illness followed the shock of my stay in the red room, but it made me nervous and I am still nervous today because of it. The doctor came to visit me.

"What made you ill yesterday?" he asked kindly.

"I was shut up in a room until after dark and there was a ghost," I told him. "And… and… I am very unhappy here. I should like to leave but I have nowhere else to go."

"Would you like to go to school?" he asked.

I hardly knew what school was, but I nodded. Nothing more was said. But one January morning, a few weeks later, I saw a carriage coming up the drive. Bessie scrubbed my face and hands and brushed my hair roughly. Then she told me to go downstairs. I stood in the hall, trembling. What a miserable creature I had become because I was always afraid!

I knocked and entered the breakfast room. I curtsied low

in front of a thin man dressed in black – a man with a face as grim as a mask. He looked me up and down.

"She is small," he said. "How old is she?"

"Ten," my aunt replied.

"Are you a good child, Jane Eyre?" the man asked.

"Perhaps the less said about that the better, Mr Brocklehurst," my aunt said when I did not answer.

"There is no sadder sight than that of a naughty child," he sighed.

"If you decide to take this child to Lowood School, Mr Brocklehurst," my aunt continued, "the teachers must keep a strict eye on her and make sure she does not tell lies. And I ask that all her holidays are spent at the school."

When Mr Brocklehurst had left, I stood there alone with my aunt.

"I must speak to her," I thought. "This will be my last chance." I went over to her and took a deep breath. "I do not tell lies," I blurted out. "If I did, I should say that I loved you! But I hate you more than anybody else in the world, except your son. I shall never come and see you when I am grown up and I shall tell everybody how cruel you have been to me."

I left Gateshead Hall four days later.

## CHAPTER TWO

# *Lowood School*

I remember little of that long journey through the wind and rain. It was dark when the carriage arrived at Lowood School. I was taken into a warm room where I met one of the teachers, Miss Temple.

"This child is very young to be sent here alone," she said to her companion. "She is tired. Give her something to eat."

I was too tired to dream that night. In the morning, a loud bell woke me up. The girls around me were getting dressed although it was still dark. I forced myself out of bed. When the bell rang again, we all walked downstairs to the classroom for prayers. At last we went into the dining room. I was so faint from hunger that I started to eat my porridge. But it was burnt and I could not finish it.

Nobody spoke to me all morning during lessons. Nobody seemed to notice me. When we went into the gloomy garden for our exercise, I saw a girl sitting on a stone seat, reading. I spoke to her. I did not know how I found the courage because I was not used to speaking to strangers. Her name was Helen Burns and we talked until the bell rang for lunch.

Lunch was a plate of potatoes and shreds of meat. At five o'clock we ate half a slice of bread and drank a cup of coffee.

After study, we were allowed a glass of water, followed by prayers and bed. Such was my first day at Lowood School.

And each day was the same – except for a visit from Mr Brocklehurst. I trembled when I saw him again, remembering what my aunt had told him. I sat at the back of the class, holding my chalk and slate carefully as I did my sums. Then suddenly, the slate slipped from my hands.

"Let the girl with the broken slate come out here!" Mr Brocklehurst shouted.

I was paralysed with fear, but the girls next to me pushed me to my feet. Mr Brocklehurst made me stand on a stool.

"This girl looks like a child," he began, "but she is really the devil. You must not speak to her! This girl is a liar!"

He left and I had to stand there until the bell rang for supper. I was so ashamed that I could hardly breathe. Helen walked past and smiled at me kindly. When the bell rang, I threw myself to the ground and wept.

"I have tried to be good," I sobbed. "I have worked hard. I want to make friends and to win their respect. I cannot bear to be hated!"

Helen brought me some bread and coffee, but I could not swallow and I went on crying.

"Jane," she said gently, "nobody likes Mr Brocklehurst. Some of the teachers and pupils may be unfriendly for a day or two, but they will soon forget what he has said."

My first three months at the school seemed to last for ever. I struggled every day to get used to new rules and I feared failure all the time. Until March, deep snow blocked the roads and we did not go beyond the school garden, except to church.

Spring came at last. Then we were allowed to take our walks beyond the gardens.

I could see that Lowood School lay in a valley by a stream, but I did not see how unhealthy this was. Spring breathed a deadly illness called typhus through our crowded schoolroom. Soon, over half the girls lay ill, weakened already by cold and lack of food. Many were sent home to die, and others died at school.

Fear now filled the school corridors. I stayed well and I even enjoyed the beauty of the season because there were no lessons. We had more food because there were fewer pupils to feed. But one worry haunted my mind. Helen Burns was ill, not with typhus, but with a disease of the lungs. By June, my dear friend was dead.

I remained at Lowood School for eight more years – six as a pupil and two as a teacher. My aunt never sent for me once, nor did she write to me. By the time I was eighteen, I was tired of the routine of Lowood. I wanted to see new people, to experience new things. Secretly, I applied for a job. And that is how I came to be a governess at Thornfield Hall.

## CHAPTER THREE

# A Cry in the Attic

It is a very strange experience to be alone in the world when you are so young. I wanted adventure, but I was afraid at the same time. As the carriage took me towards my new home at Thornfield Hall, I had plenty of time to think.

"I only pray that Mrs Fairfax who has employed me does not turn out to be like my aunt," I thought to myself. "But if the worst comes to the worst, I can leave."

Thornfield Hall was outside a small village. The house was in darkness when I arrived, except for one candlelit room. Inside that room was a cheerful fire. Mrs Fairfax was a little elderly lady dressed in black. A cat sat at her feet and she was knitting. I felt happier.

"Shall I meet Miss Fairfax tonight?" I asked her.

She looked puzzled. "Oh, you mean Miss Varens!" she said.

"Then my pupil is not your daughter?" I asked.

"No."

I did not ask any more questions. I did not want to seem rude. We talked for some time and when I went to my room I felt happy and safe at last. In the morning, I got up early and walked in the gardens. There I met Mrs Fairfax again.

"Thornfield Hall is a pretty place," she said. "I wish that Mr Rochester would live here all the time."

"Mr Rochester?" I asked. "Who is he?"

"The owner," she replied. "He is guardian to little Adele Varens, your pupil. She has just come here from France with her nurse."

As she spoke, a girl ran across the lawn. She was about seven or eight, small and pale with curly hair falling to her waist. She was polite to me and I spoke in French to her, to put her at ease. When we had eaten breakfast, she sang to me and recited a poem that her mother had taught her before her death. I taught Adele only in the morning. That afternoon, Mrs Fairfax showed me around the house.

"Mr Rochester's visits are rare," she told me. "I never know when he will arrive, so I have to keep the rooms ready."

"Do you like him?" I asked.

"I have no reason not to like him," she replied. "But I do not always know whether he is serious or not when he speaks."

We reached some small rooms at the top of the house. From there, we walked out onto the roof. The view was wonderful. As I came back down and wandered along the corridor, I suddenly heard a laugh. It stopped. Then it began again, even louder. Mrs Fairfax caught up with me. "One of the servants," she explained, "probably Grace Poole. I often hear her. She sews in one of these rooms."

As she spoke, the laugh sounded again. It was unhappy and chilled me. The door nearest me opened and a woman came out – she had red hair and a hard face.

"Too much noise, Grace Poole!" Mrs Fairfax called out.

I often went up to the roof to enjoy the view – and I often heard Grace Poole's laugh. Sometimes, she spoke in a low voice, although I could not understand what she was saying.

One afternoon in January, Adele was ill and I agreed to let her have the day in bed. It was a fine but very cold day. I offered to post a letter for Mrs Fairfax because I wanted to walk. About a mile from Thornfield Hall, and half way to the village, I sat down to rest on a stile. I stayed there until the sun sank crimson behind the trees and the moon was rising. The noise of a horse broke the silence. Suddenly, it slipped on a sheet of ice, throwing its rider to the ground. I ran over to him.

"Are you injured, sir?" I asked. "I can fetch help from Thornfield Hall."

"No thank you," he replied. "I have no broken bones. Only a sprained ankle."

I could see him clearly in the moonlight. He was a man of about thirty-five, with a tanned, stern face and heavy eyebrows. I offered again to go for help.

"Do you know Mr Rochester?" he asked.

"No," I replied. "I have never seen him."

"Are you…?" he stopped and looked at my simple black clothes.

"I am the governess there," I told him.

He set off again, leading his horse and his dog by his side – and I went to post my letter. When I returned to Thornfield Hall, there was a fire burning brightly in Mrs Fairfax's room – but no Mrs Fairfax. Instead, all alone, sitting on the rug gazing at the fire was a great black and white dog like the one I had just seen in the lane. It got up and came to me, wagging its tail. A servant entered the room.

"Whose dog is this?" I asked her.

"Pilot?" she replied. "He has just arrived with Mr Rochester. His master fell from his horse on the way here."

"So I have met the master of Thornfield Hall at last!" I told myself.

## CHAPTER FOUR

# *Fire! Fire!*

I did not meet Mr Rochester again until the following afternoon when he invited myself, and Adele, to tea. I was nervous because I was not used to strangers. Mr Rochester was sitting by the fire, his foot resting on a cushion. He was staring at his dog and Adele.

"Let Miss Eyre be seated," he said, not looking up as Mrs Fairfax showed me in.

Mr Rochester took his tea in silence. Then suddenly he started to ask me questions.

"Eight years!" he said, when I told him about Lowood School. "No wonder you look as if you come from another world. Adele has already shown me some of your sketches. Show me some more, Miss Eyre."

I fetched them and he studied them carefully. They were nothing special, reader – water colours of clouds and sea and hills and icebergs.

"You have not enough artist's skill," he said at last. "But even so, they are unusual drawings for a schoolgirl. Now put them away and take Adele to bed."

"He is a strange, rude man." I said to Mrs Fairfax when I came back downstairs.

"I am used to his ways," she replied. "It is partly his nature. But he also has painful thoughts."

I was not satisfied by her answer, but I understood that she did not want me to ask any more questions. I saw little of Mr Rochester during the next few days, until he had visitors to dine. When they had gone, he sent for me again. He was smiling and his eyes sparkled.

"Do you think I am handsome, Miss Jane?" he asked.

"No, sir," I told him.

"And you are not pretty," he said. "I need company tonight. I want to learn more about you. So speak!"

"What about, sir?"

"Whatever you choose," he replied.

I said nothing.

"You are dumb, Miss Eyre, or stubborn."

"I do not know what will interest you, sir," I said at last.

But we went on to talk of many things and we often talked after that. I felt less shy with him – as if he were a relation more than my master. I became happier, plumper and healthier. And did I still think he was ugly? No, reader, I did not. However, I did not forget his faults. He was still harsh, bossy and moody – but I believed that he could not help it.

One night, at two o'clock in the morning, I woke up suddenly. I heard a sound outside my door.

"Who is there?" I called out.

There was no answer. I turned cold with fear.

"Perhaps it is Pilot," I told myself.

I tried to sleep again, but I heard a laugh – low and deep – right outside my door. Then something gurgled and moaned. Was it Grace Poole? I could no longer remain alone. I picked up my candle and opened the door to call Mrs Fairfax. To my surprise, the corridor was filled with smoke coming from under Mr Rochester's door. I ran into his room and found that the curtains around his bed were on fire.

"Wake up! Wake up!" I cried, shaking him. But the smoke had made him sleepy. I threw a jug of water over the bed to put out the flames.

"Are you trying to drown me, Jane Eyre?" he asked, opening his eyes at last.

I told him what had happened and he listened in silence.

"Stay here," he said. "Do not call anyone. I must go up to the attic."

I did as he asked.

"As you guessed, it was Grace Poole," he told me when he came back. "You have saved my life, Miss Eyre, and I am in your debt. I cannot say anymore."

I returned to my room, but I did not try to sleep. And I got up as soon as day broke.

I waited all day to see Mr Rochester, but he did not send for me, or Adele. When darkness fell, I thought I heard his footsteps and I turned to the door, expecting to see him. But the door remained shut. I had so many things to ask him about the night before! At last, Mrs Fairfax brought in the tea.

"Mr Rochester has good weather for his journey," she said, looking through the window.

"I did not know he was out," I replied.

"He set off after breakfast," Mrs Fairfax replied. "He has been invited to stay with friends. There will be a large party. I think he will stay a week or more."

"Will there be ladies there?" I asked.

"Yes, Lord Ingram's daughters," she told me. "I met Blanche Ingram a few years ago, when she was eighteen."

"What is she like?"

"Tall and beautiful, with a long graceful neck and large black eyes," Mrs Fairfax replied. "And the glossiest curls I have ever seen. She has a beautiful voice. She and Mr Rochester sang a duet together."

"You are a plain and poor governess, Jane Eyre," I told myself when I was alone. "You may be falling in love with Mr Rochester, but do not imagine that he could be interested in *you*."

I decided to make two sketches – one of me, poor and plain, and one of the beautiful Miss Ingram.

"And whenever I think that my master might like me, I shall compare them to remind me," I thought.

Ten days passed and Mr Rochester did not return. I was disappointed, but I spoke firmly to myself. "You are only a governess, Jane Eyre. You have *nothing* to do with the master of Thornfield Hall!"

# CHAPTER FIVE

# *An Unwelcome Visitor*

On a mild April day, Mr Rochester returned, bringing his visitors with him, including Miss Ingram. I went downstairs with Adele that evening when she was introduced to the ladies. I found Miss Ingram as beautiful as the painting I had made, but hard and haughty. At last, just before the gentlemen came back into the room, I slipped out through the side-door. There I came face to face with Mr Rochester.

"Return to the drawing-room, Miss Eyre," he said kindly.

"I am tired, sir," I replied.

"And a little depressed?" he asked. "I can see the tears shining in your eyes. But as long as my visitors are here, I must ask you to appear here every evening."

The days that followed were happy ones for Thornfield Hall. All sad feelings seem to leave the house. It was alive. But Mr Rochester did not notice me. And now that I had learnt to love him, I could not *unlove* him! I realised that he would marry Miss Ingram – although she did not charm him.

One evening, when Mr Rochester was in the village on business, a stranger arrived. He was a tall, fine-looking man – and very polite.

"My name is Mr Mason," he told Mrs Fairfax. "I must

wait for your master as I have travelled all the way from the West Indies to see him."

I was standing in the hall when Mr Rochester returned. "There is a Mr Mason waiting for you, sir," I told him. "From Jamaica."

The smile froze on his lips as he caught hold of my arm. He sat down, trembling, and held my hand.

"My little friend," he said. "I wish I were on a quiet island with only you. I wish that all trouble and danger would disappear." He took a sip of water. "Show Mason here," he said, "and then leave me."

That night, I forgot to draw my curtains. When the moon rose, full and bright, it woke me up. Suddenly, a wild cry ran from one end of Thornfield Hall to the other. My heart almost stopped beating at the sound. Then I heard noise and shouting above my room. "Help! Help! Help!" a voice called. "Will nobody come to help me? Rochester, for God's sake! Help me!"

I dressed quickly and ran into the corridor. Our visitors were awake, too. The door at the end of the corridor opened and Mr Rochester came towards us, holding up a candle. Miss Ingram seized his arm.

"What terrible thing has happened?" she asked.

"A servant has had a nightmare," he said. "That is all. I ask you all to go back to sleep."

A few minutes later, Mr Rochester tapped on my door. "I

need your help," he whispered. "Come with me, quietly. And bring a cloth. You do not mind the sight of blood?"

"I do not know," I replied. "I do not think so."

He led me to a room I had first visited with Mrs Fairfax. But the tapestry on the wall was now pulled back to reveal a door. It was open. I heard a snarl, like the sound of a dog. Mr Rochester went in and I heard a laugh.

"Grace Poole is in there!" I thought.

He called me in. On a chair sat Mr Mason, his eyes

closed, his face pale – and his arm soaked with blood.

"You must stay with him until I return with a doctor," Mr Rochester said. "Clean up the blood and give him water to sip."

I sat there until the candle went out. Just before dawn, I heard Pilot barking and Mr Rochester entered the room with a doctor.

"She bit me!" Mr Mason groaned as he opened his eyes. "But Rochester got the knife from her." He trembled. "It was terrible," he whispered. "She was like a tigress. She sucked my blood."

I shuddered at his words.

"You should not have tried to see her alone," Mr Rochester said. "I warned you."

His face showed horror and disgust. "You must go back to Jamaica and forget her."

When day began to dawn, we helped Mr Mason into a carriage. As it drove away, Mr Rochester walked towards the garden. The sun was shining on the dew and he picked a rose.

"Jane, you have had a strange night," he said. "Will you accept this flower?"

"Thank you, sir," I replied. "Will you still allow Grace Poole to live here?"

"Oh, yes," he said. "But you *must* forget about her, Jane."

## CHAPTER SIX

# *Forgive and Forget*

The following day, Mrs Fairfax sent for me. A man, dressed in black, was waiting to speak to me.

"You will not remember me, Miss Eyre," he said. "I am your aunt's coachman at Gateshead Hall."

"I do remember you, Robert!" I cried. "You married Bessie. How is she?"

"Well, Miss," he replied. "We have three children now. But I cannot give you good news of your family. Mr John died last week. He lived a wicked life. Mrs Reed is very ill with the shock of it. She keeps saying your name, Miss. She wants me to take you back with me."

"I ought to go," I said. "I shall speak to Mr Rochester."

I found him with Miss Ingram and the others. He was not pleased to let me go and made me promise to return as soon as I could.

"But if you marry Miss Ingram," I said, "Adele ought to go away to school. You will have no need of me."

"Promise me, Jane, that you will not look for a new job," he said. "Not yet."

"I promise, sir," I replied.

I reached Gateshead Hall at five o'clock in the afternoon

on the first of May. I visited Bessie. Then I walked up the drive to the big house. It was almost nine years since I had walked down this drive that dark January morning. I felt stronger now and less afraid.

I went inside and talked politely for some time to my cousins. Then they showed me into my aunt's bedroom. I had left her in bitterness and hate. Now I was sorry that she suffered so greatly. I wanted to forget and forgive the past. I went over to the bed. Her face was still stern as I leaned over to kiss her.

"Are you Jane Eyre?" she asked.

"Yes, Aunt Reed," I replied. "How are you, dear aunt?"

I took her hand, but she pulled it away and looked at me coldly.

"I had more trouble with Jane Eyre than anybody would believe," she said. "I was glad when she left. I wish she had died at Lowood."

"A strange wish, Mrs Reed," I replied angrily. "Why do you hate her so much?"

"I always disliked her mother," my aunt said. "She was my husband's only sister and his great favourite. When she died, he wept like a fool and sent for the baby. I hated it – a sickly, whining thing!"

She fell into a deep sleep and it was ten days before we were able to speak again. Then she made me read this letter:

*Madeira*
*The Canary Isles*

*Madam,*

*Will you please send me the address of my niece, Jane Eyre? I wish to write to her to ask her to come and live with me. I wish also to adopt her.*

*Yours, John Eyre*

"My father's brother!" I said. Then I looked at the date. "It was written three years ago! Why did I not receive it?"

"I hated you," my aunt replied. "I wrote back to him and

told him that you had died of typhus fever at Lowood School."

"I tried to love you, aunt," I cried. I leaned over her. "Will you kiss me now?" She refused. "Love me or hate me," I said, "but I forgive you."

A few weeks after her death, I set out for Thornfield Hall again. I had not told anyone the exact date of my return because I did not wish the carriage to meet me in the village. I wanted to walk up to the house alone.

It was a dull June evening when I arrived. As I walked between the rose-filled hedges, I saw the narrow stile where I had first met my master – and there he was! I trembled when I saw him and turned to go another way, but he had already seen me.

"Hello!" he cried. "There you are!"

"I am pleased to be back," I told him.

We walked back to the house together. Little Adele was wild with joy when she saw me. A fortnight of calm followed my return. Mr Rochester said nothing of his marriage and I saw no preparations for it. He did not visit Miss Ingram and she did not visit him.

And during that time, he sent for me many times to talk to him. He had never been kinder to me – and I had never loved him so much.

## CHAPTER SEVEN

# The Face in the Candlelight

On Midsummer's Eve, I went out into the garden to sit in the orchard by the light of the rising moon. The sky was blue and the air warm and I could smell the sweet jasmine and honeysuckle. When I heard my master's footsteps on the path, I hoped that he would not see me. But he called me and asked me to sit with him.

"It is a shame to sit in the house on such a beautiful night," he said.

I started to talk about his coming marriage and I could not stop myself from weeping.

"I wish I had never been born!" I cried. "I wish I had never come here! I love Thornfield Hall. I have lived a happy life here. And I am filled with terror at the thought of leaving you."

"Why must you leave?" he asked, surprised.

His words angered me. "Do you think I have no feelings?" I cried. "If I had been rich and beautiful, you would want *me*, not Miss Ingram."

Mr Rochester put his arms around me and kissed me. "I offer *you* my heart, Jane," he said.

"Do not laugh at me, sir, I beg you," I replied.

"Will you marry me, Jane?" he asked.

I froze on the spot in amazement.

"Miss Ingram does not love me!" he shouted. "And I do not love her."

I thought hard for a long time. "Yes, I shall marry you," I said at last.

As I spoke, rain began to fall and we rushed back to the house. But I slept soundly in spite of a great storm. In the morning, I wondered if I had dreamed it all. But Mr Rochester talked of nothing but our marriage. Mrs Fairfax was cold towards me.

"You are so young and inexperienced in life," she said. "I fear that you will be disappointed. Gentlemen do not usually marry governesses."

But I was happy. My future husband was becoming my whole world. The preparations for our wedding day were made and everything was packed for our honeymoon to Europe. The evening before our wedding, Mr Rochester returned from a visit to one of his farms. I could not eat anything.

"What is wrong, Jane?" he asked. "Tell me! Are you nervous?"

"A strange thing happened last night," I told him. "A howling noise woke me up. I heard it above the wind. And when I fell asleep, I dreamed that Thornfield Hall was in ruins and that you were riding away from it. Then I woke up again. Somebody was holding a candle over me. I did not recognise the face that looked down at me."

"What did she look like, Jane?" he asked.

"She was tall with long dark hair," I replied. "She took my wedding veil and put it on her head and turned to the mirror." I trembled. "I have never seen such a face! It was wild, with blood-shot eyes. She ripped my veil to pieces. As she turned to go, she held the candle closer to my face… and… I fainted. Tell me, sir! Who was she?"

"Nobody," he said, "but in your imagination."

"She was real!" I protested.

Mr Rochester took me in his arms and comforted me.

"And my veil is torn to pieces," I said.

I felt Mr Rochester shudder. "That woman must have been Grace Poole," he said. "You saw what she did to poor Mason. She seemed worse because you were half asleep. You must wonder why I keep such a woman in my house. I shall tell you when we have been married a year and a day. I promise. Will you agree, Jane?"

I nodded.

"Now go to bed and dream of happy love," he said.

As I entered the church the next day, I saw two strangers lurking in the churchyard. Our marriage service began. As is the custom, the clergyman asked if there was any reason why we should not be married. He paused, not expecting a reply, and carried on with the ceremony. Then a man's voice rang out in that small church. "This marriage cannot take place. Mr Rochester already has a wife."

## CHAPTER EIGHT

# *Alone*

I did not faint at these words. I looked at Mr Rochester and I made him look at me. His face had lost all colour.

The voice went on. "Fifteen years ago, Mr Rochester was married to Bertha Mason in Jamaica."

"It is true. I *have* been married," Mr Rochester replied at last. "But that does not mean my wife is still alive."

"She was three months ago," the man said. "Step forward, Mr Mason."

At this name, Mr Rochester trembled with anger from head to toe. He lifted his arm and I thought he would strike him.

"I am Bertha's brother," Mason said. "I saw her at Thornfield Hall."

A grim smile twisted Mr Rochester's lips. "There will be no wedding today," he said. "Bertha Mason *is* my wife. But she is mad. She comes from a mad family. But they did not tell me their secret. They let me marry her." He looked around the church. "Now I invite you all to come up to the house and meet – my wife! You will judge whether I was right or not to break my marriage vows."

And clutching me to him, we left the church for

Thornfield Hall. We reached the house and went up to the attic. Mr Rochester lifted the tapestry from the wall and unlocked the door behind. In a room without a window sat Grace Poole, bent over the fire, cooking.

At the far end of the room, a figure ran backwards and forwards. Whether it was an animal or a human being it was not possible to tell. It ran on all fours, growling like a wild animal, black hair hiding its face. A fierce cry greeted Mr Rochester's voice and the creature stood up on two legs.

"Take care, sir!" Grace Poole said.

The creature came forward and I recognised her face. *She* had come to my room and torn my wedding veil! She sprang at Mr Rochester and gripped him by the throat, biting his cheek. At last, he grabbed her hands and tied them together.

He turned towards us. "That is my wife," he said. He put a hand on my shoulder. "And this is the wife I should like. Be off with you now, gentlemen. I must lock up my wife again."

I walked slowly down the stairs with Mr Mason and his lawyer, the man who had spoken out in the church.

"Your uncle, Mr Eyre, has worked for my family company in Madeira for many years," Mr Mason told me. "I was with him when your letter arrived telling him of your marriage to Rochester."

When everybody had left, I locked the door to my room and wept. Then I took off my wedding dress and put on my old dress. I was a lonely, cold girl again. A winter frost had come in mid-summer. My hopes of a happy life had gone. I longed for death.

Later that afternoon, as the sun began to sink, I realised that nobody had come to my door – not Adele, or Mrs Fairfax or Mr Rochester. I unbolted my door and went outside. Mr Rochester was sitting outside my room.

"Well, Jane," he said. "Will you ever forgive me?"

Reader! I forgave him on the spot! But only in my heart, not in words.

"I *do* love you," I said, "more than ever. But I must not show it. You are a married man. This is the last time I shall tell you so. I must leave Thornfield Hall. I must leave you forever and start a new life."

"I shall be unhappy when you have left," he said sadly. "What shall I do, Jane?" He let go of me. "Remember, you leave me in agony, Jane. Remember my suffering when you have gone. My life has been hell until now. But for the first time, I am truly in love."

He kissed my forehead gently. I went back towards my room.

"You are really leaving me?" he asked.

"Yes," I said. I walked back to him and kissed his cheek. "God bless you, master!" I whispered.

Then I left him. "Farewell!" I thought. "Farewell for ever!"

## CHAPTER NINE

# *A Voice in the Dark*

I left Thornfield Hall before dawn. I walked past fields and hedgerows, weeping, my shoes wet with dew. I was so weak with unhappiness that I stopped to lie on the ground. As I got to my feet again, a coach stopped for me. I offered the driver all the money I had and climbed inside.

Two days later, the coach dropped me at a crossroads called Whitcross in the north of England. It was dusk and I could see the shape of the moors beyond. I set off towards them, walking through deep heather. It was a warm night and I gathered berries to eat. Then I lay down in the heather to sleep.

The next morning, I went back to the crossroads and began to walk along the road until I heard a church bell in the distance. At two o'clock, I entered a village. I knocked on many doors, offering to exchange my gloves for a piece of bread. But everybody refused. I returned to the moor.

"I should rather die up here than in a pauper's grave," I told myself.

As I looked around me, I saw a light on a far hill. Rain began to fall and I decided to try to reach it. Reader, when I came to Moor House, they took me in! I should have died on the moor if they had not. The more I knew of the clergyman who lived there –Mr Rivers – and his two sisters, Diana and Mary, the more I came to like them. I called myself Jane Elliott. Mr Rivers opened a small village school for girls, and it was here that I found my new home.

"Have I done the right thing?" I asked myself. "Which is better? To love Mr Rochester and live in luxury and be ashamed of what I have done? Or to be a village schoolmistress – honest and free?"

I knew that I had chosen the right path.

One November evening, Mr Rivers came to see me. "Come and sit by the fire," he said, "and listen to my story. I heard it from my solicitor. It is about a poor clergyman who fell in love with a rich girl. They married and had a baby daughter. Then they both died. The child's uncle, a Mr Reed, took her in. She lived for ten unhappy years there. She became a teacher like you. Then she became a governess to a Mr Rochester. He promised to marry her, but he had a mad wife locked up at the top of his house." He looked at me. "It is a strange story, isn't it?"

"Since you have found out so much, tell me!" I said. "How is Mr Rochester?"

"I do not know," he replied. "My friend's letter does not mention him. But you should be asking the name of the governess," he said. "And since you do not, I shall tell you. Jane Eyre. Am I right?"

"Yes, yes," I replied.

"You do not wonder why this solicitor is searching for you?" he asked. "Your uncle, John Eyre, has died in Madeira. He has left you all his money. You are rich."

"But why did he write to you and not to me?" I asked.

"He also found out that I am your cousin," he said. "My mother was your father's sister."

"Oh, I am so glad!" I said. "I had nobody and now I have three relations!"

I had the happiest Christmas I have ever had at Moor House with my new family. But I did not forget Mr Rochester, not for a single moment. I wanted to know what had happened to him. I wrote to Mrs Fairfax, but I received no reply.

As winter became spring and then summer, I felt sad. Mr Rivers had decided to go to India as a missionary and he begged me to go with him as his wife. I refused. He begged me again.

"I can only marry you if that is God's will," I told him. "I shall pray now."

The candle in the room was dying out and the room was full of moonlight as I knelt down. My heart was beating fast. As I finished praying, I heard a faint voice, crying and full of pain.

"I heard a voice, Jane!" Mr Rivers said. "What did it say?"

I had heard the voice, too. It was not the voice of God, but of a human being. It was a well-known and beloved voice. It was the voice of Edward Rochester.

"Wait for me! I will come to you!" I cried back.

# CHAPTER TEN

# *"Reader, I married him!"*

I got up as soon as it was light. It was the first day of June, but it was cold and raining. As I waited for the coach at the crossroads, I heard its wheels rumbling in the distance.

"It is a year since the same carriage dropped me here a year ago!" I whispered. "What a poor and unhappy creature I was then."

The journey to Thornfield Hall took me a day and a half. I ran from the lane, desperate for my first glimpse of the house. I came to the orchard, where Mr Rochester had asked me to marry him. I looked across to the house.

But it wasn't there. I could see only a ruin, as I had seen it in my dream before my wedding day. And there was the silence of death around it. I ran all the way to the village inn.

"Is Mr Rochester living at Thornfield Hall?" I asked, although I knew the answer.

"No, ma'am," the innkeeper replied. "I suppose you are a stranger or you would have heard what happened. It was last autumn. Fire broke out in the middle of the night. It was a terrible sight. I watched it myself."

"Who started the fire?" I asked.

"They think it was the mad woman he kept there," the

man replied. "Grace Poole had too much to drink one night. The mad woman took her keys and got out. They say she nearly burnt her husband in his bed once, but the governess saved him."

"And Mr Rochester?" I asked. "Was he there?"

"Yes!" the man said. "He never left the house except at night. Then he wandered like a ghost in the orchard. He went upstairs when the fire started and got all the servants out. Then he went to save his mad wife, too. But she was up on the roof. I saw her, screaming and waving. Mr Rochester called her name. She heard him and jumped. She was smashed to pieces below."

"Good God!" I cried. "Were…Did anybody else die?"

"No," he said. "But it would have been better if they had."

"What do you mean?"

"He is blind," he replied. "Mr Edward Rochester is alive, but blind. The ceiling crashed on him as he came down the staircase. He lost a hand as well."

"Where is he?" I cried.

"On one of his farms – about thirty miles from here," he explained.

I ordered a coach immediately and I arrived just as it was getting dark. The farmhouse was dark and gloomy, and the sound of the rain in the trees was the only sound in that lonely place. The door opened slowly and a man came out into the twilight. He put out his hand to feel the rain.

It was my master, Edward Rochester.

I stood still, holding my breath and watching him. His face had a desperate and brooding look that reminded me of a caged bird. He opened his eyes and gazed blankly towards the sky. Then he went back into the house.

His servant showed me into the sitting room. It was dark in spite of the fire. When I went in, Pilot, his old dog, pricked up his ears and yelped.

"Down, Pilot," I said quietly.

"Who is this?" Mr Rochester asked, putting out his hands to try to find me. "Speak!"

"Pilot knows me," I replied.

He put out his hand again and I held it. He caught hold of my arm, my neck and my waist. "Is it Jane?" he asked.

"Yes, my dear master," I replied. "I am Jane Eyre. I have found you and I have come back to you. I am a rich woman now. I shall look after you."

Mr Rochester sighed. "No, Jane," he said.

We talked for many days. I told him of my life at Moor House, my school – and Mr Rivers.

"I want you to choose, Jane," he said, "and I will accept your decision. Will you marry me, a poor blind crippled man twenty years older than you?"

"Yes, sir," I replied at once.

"May God bless you!" he whispered. "I have begun to pray, Jane. Briefly. Last Monday night, I begged God to let me die. I thought you must be dead and I wanted to be with you again. I called out your name."

"I know," I whispered. "I heard you."

Reader, I married him! I have been married for ten years now and I have never been happier. Two years after our marriage, Mr Rochester recovered the sight of one eye. Dear Diana and Mary Rivers both married and we see them every year. Mr Rivers went to India where he still lives, but he never married. And Adele? She has left school now and is our dearest companion.